ALLIE'S WORLD
Block Party

MARIMBA BOOKS
An imprint of The Hudson Publishing Group LLC
356 Glenwood Avenue, East Orange, New Jersey

Text copyright © 2011 by Karen Valentin. Illustrations copyright © 2011 by Michelle Dorenkamp.

Special book excerpts or customized printings can also be created to fit specific needs.

For details write or phone the office of the Marimba special sales manager.
Marimba Books, 356 Glenwood Avenue, East Orange, New Jersey 07017, 973 672-7701.

MARIMBA BOOKS and the Marimba Books logo are trademarks of
The Hudson Publishing Group LLC.

ISBN-13: 978 1-60349-017-7   ISBN-10: 1-60349-017-5

10 9 8 7 6 5 4 3 2 1

Printed in Canada

Wake up Allie," **Mami** said. "Today is the big block party!"

Every year my family and neighbors have a great big party on our street. I've been waiting a long time. But the day is finally here!

Tio Danny and **Abuelo** came early to help **Papi** bring the tables and chairs outside.

Abuela and **Tia** Nancy helped **Mami** make food for the party.

Mami put on the morning news. "Let's hear the weather report," she said.

The weatherman pointed to a picture of raindrops and a big dark cloud. "Enjoy the sunshine while you can," he said. "It looks like a rainstorm is coming our way."

"A rainstorm?" I screamed. "What about the block party?"

"It's not raining yet," **Abuela** said, looking out the window. "Let's enjoy the sunshine and the party while we can."

We quickly packed the food and set up the table in front of our apartment building.

"Good morning," said our neighbor Mrs. Ling. Her table was already filled with food. "Be sure to try some of my homemade egg rolls before the rainstorm comes."

The sun was still shining when my friends ran up to me. "Come and play with us Allie!" they said.

We jumped rope and we played hopscotch, freeze tag, and hide and seek. Soon we were hot and sweaty.

We changed into our bathing suits and Eddie took the cap off the fire hydrant.

He made a big fountain with the water.
My friends and I ran from one side to
the other. It was just like a rainstorm,
but the sun was still shining.

When I finished playing in the water, **Mami** served me lunch. Since all the neighbors share their food, I had many different things to eat on my plate.

"Do you like it?" Mrs. Ling asked me when she saw me eating one of her egg rolls.

"It's delicious," I answered.

After lunch, I heard the **piragua** man ring his bell. **Papi** gave me money and I ran to the little cart.

"What flavor?" he asked.

"Cherry please," I said, giving him a dollar.

The **piragua** man scraped the big block of ice and filled a plastic cup with ice bits. It looked like snow. He poured cherry juice on top until the ice cone was bright red.

I ate my **piragua** while I sat on **Abuelo's** lap. He was playing dominos with his friends. Sometimes **Abuelo** lets me help him. I know how to play because he taught me.

"You see?" **Abuelo** said. "The rainstorm is waiting for you. It wants you to have a fun day."

I sipped the cherry ice with a big smile.

In the middle of the street there was a big empty stage.

One by one, musicians came up with their instruments. There were guitars, trumpets, bongos, drums, and a big piano.

One of our neighbors introduced the band. Everyone clapped as the band started to play their music.

Abuelo danced with **Abuela**, **Tio** Danny danced with **Tia** Nancy, **Papi** danced with **Mami** and I danced with all my cousins and friends.

We danced for a long time, and
soon we were all hot and sweaty.
I wished we could play in the fire
hydrant again.

Just as I was thinking that, the
dark clouds began to cover the sun.
I felt little drops of cool rain on my
face. It felt wonderful!

Abuelo was right. The rainstorm waited for me to have a fun day in the sun, and it came when I wanted to play in the water once again.

The music kept on playing and we all kept dancing in the rain.

For Matthew, Jason and Allie—KV
For Katlyn, Brandon and Bryce, with love—MD

Karen Valentin is a Puerto Rican-American writer who has authored several books including *The Flavor of Our Hispanic Faith* and *Hallway Diaries*. A graduate of Fordham University with a BA in English Literature, she is also a contributor to *Guideposts Books*. Karen lives in New York City and is the mother of two little boys. *Block Party* is the second title in her *Allie's World* picture book series. The first title is *What Did Abuela Say?*

Michelle Dorenkamp has been drawing since age three. She earned a BFA in Illustration and has since illustrated more than fifty children's books. Her work is also featured monthly in National Wildlife's *Wild Animal Baby* magazine. Michelle works from her home studio using traditional watercolors, pen and inks, markers and prismacolors as well as digital illustration. She resides in St. Louis, Missouri, and enjoys spending free time with her family, especially her granddaughter Katlyn.